TO _____

Disney's
SMALL WORLD LIBRARY
DONALD'S BURIED TREASURE
An Adventure in Greece

GROLIER ENTERPRISES INC.
DANBURY, CONNECTICUT

© 1991 The Walt Disney Company. All rights reserved. Printed in the United States of America. Developed by the Walt Disney Company in conjunction with Nancy Hall, Inc.
ISBN: 0-7172-8233-3

On the deck of the cruise ship *Triton*, Donald Duck studied a map of the Greek isles.

"This cruise isn't going to be long enough," Donald complained. "We aren't visiting even half the Greek islands. I want to see them all!"

"But there are hundreds of islands, Donald," Daisy said. "Isn't it better to spend time on a few of them than rushing around trying to see them all?"

Donald shook his head. "When I do something, I like to do it right."

Daisy sighed. "You mean, you think you're always right."

That afternoon, Captain Pappas gathered all the *Triton*'s passengers on deck.

"Here is your chance to live like Greeks!" the captain announced to the passengers. "Our country is mostly made up of islands surrounded by three seas. Fishing is a way of life for many Greek people."

The crew began to pass out fishing poles to the passengers. "Tonight is Catch-Your-Own-Dinner Night," Captain Pappas concluded. "Enjoy yourselves—and good luck!"

Daisy baited her hook and cast her line into the sea.

Donald was in such a hurry, he got tangled in his fishing line. "How am I supposed to catch a fish this way?" he complained. "There's something wrong with the pole they gave me."

"You can share the fish I catch," Daisy offered.

"Never mind," Donald said, untangling himself. "I'm going to catch the biggest fish of all! After all, there's no point in fishing if you can't catch the biggest fish."

TRITON

A few minutes later, Donald felt a mighty tug on his fishing line. A huge swordfish thrashed on the other end of the line.

"Help!" Donald shrieked.

"It's too big! Let go of the fishing pole!" Daisy called.

But Donald stubbornly tightened his grip. Within seconds the fish pulled him right off the deck and into the sea.

When the *Triton*'s crew pulled him back on board, Donald was covered with wiggly octopuses.

"Delicious!" Captain Pappas cried. "You have made the best catch of all. Octopuses are a delicacy in Greece. Of course, you do have an unusual method of catching them," he told an embarrassed Donald.

The next morning the *Triton* pulled into the port at Rhodes.

"This is going to be great," said Donald happily, rubbing his hands together. "I've heard that bargaining is the way to shop in Greece. Wait until you see me in action."

"Please don't get carried away," Daisy cautioned.

But as soon as they reached the marketplace, Donald began arguing with a merchant selling handmade pottery. Daisy just sighed and went off shopping on her own.

At lunchtime Daisy went back to the first stall, only to find Donald still arguing. "You should pay me to take this vase!" Donald told the merchant.

The crowd that had gathered around Donald burst out laughing at Donald's bargaining skills.

Daisy scolded Donald. "Don't you think it would have been more fun to tour the marketplace instead of arguing all morning? That seems like a poor bargain to me."

Donald tried to say something, but his throat was too sore.

After lunch, the cruise passengers visited the Valley of the Butterflies.

"It's amazing!" Daisy whispered. At a glance the peaceful valley seemed deserted. But when she looked more closely, Daisy could see hundreds of butterflies clinging to the shady trees.

Zena, the tour guide, clapped her hands, and the butterflies suddenly fluttered into the sky. They circled above in a beautiful swirling cloud. Then the butterflies settled back down, their folded wings blending into the tree bark.

"That looks like fun!" said Donald. Before Daisy could
stop him, Donald began clapping his hands, again and
again. Soon all the butterflies flew away.

Daisy sighed. "When will you learn that enough is
enough?"

"The ancient Greeks believed in moderation in all
things," Zena told Donald gently.

"Moderation?" Donald asked.

"Not too little, not too much," Zena explained. "One
piece of candy tastes good. But if you eat a whole box,
you will feel sick."

"Not me!" Donald said.

Next Zena led the tour group to a restaurant where music was being played. Donald didn't feel like dancing, but Daisy couldn't resist the lively Greek music. She was soon stepping and swaying with the crowd.

"Come on, Donald. It's fun!" Daisy called.

Half the people in the restaurant were up and dancing. The others clapped their hands and snapped their fingers. Suddenly a plate crashed to the floor, then another, and another.

"What's going on?" Daisy asked in alarm.

"It's a Greek tradition. That's how Greeks show they like the dancing," explained Zena. "You are a very good dancer."

Happy patrons threw more plates, and everyone cheered.

"I'm a good dancer, too!" Donald declared. He jumped up to join the dance. "They'll throw even more plates for me!" he said to himself.

But Donald tried so hard to get all the steps right, he couldn't take his eyes off his own feet. Daisy looked up just in time to see Donald heading straight toward a waiter carrying a tray full of food.

"Look out!" she called.

But it was too late. Donald crashed into the waiter and
fell to the ground, covered with food.

"Your cucumber and yogurt salad sure looks good!" he
said sheepishly.

The next stop on the cruise was Platomon. There the group boarded a bus to take them to Olympia, site of the ancient Olympic Games.

"This is where the Olympic Games started," Zena told them when they reached the beautiful stadium. "Exercise was very important to the ancient Greeks. They believed that the mind works best in a healthy body."

Donald fidgeted as Zena spoke. He knew that Triton Tours had scheduled its own Olympic Games, and he couldn't wait to get started. "I'll win plenty of medals to bring back home!" he thought happily.

When the entry sheets were passed around, Donald
signed up for every event.

"Don't you think that's too much?" Daisy asked.

"Of course not!" said Donald. "Now I can win more
than anyone else!"

"What happened to moderation?" Daisy asked him.

"That's for the ancient Greeks," Donald scoffed.

Donald ran from the finish line of one event to the starting line of the next. But since he had entered so many contests, he was too tired to win any of them.

Captain Pappas gave out prizes of wreaths made from laurel leaves, just like the ones given at the first Olympic Games.

"And the prize for 'Most Events Entered' goes to Donald Duck," the captain announced.

Donald staggered up to the captain. He was so exhausted he couldn't even stand.

The next day Zena announced that the passengers were invited to visit a special site where they could learn how to assist archaeologists on a dig.

At the site, Zena introduced the group to Dr. Theopolis, an archaeologist from a nearby museum. "Dr. Theopolis will show you the proper way to dig for ancient objects," said Zena.

Dr. Theopolis began to explain certain techniques to the group, as he handed out the shovels. Donald couldn't wait to begin, and he immediately started to dig.

"Don't you want to listen to the archaeologist, so you'll know how to dig?" Daisy asked.

"I already know how to dig," Donald scoffed, tossing dirt over his shoulder. "Besides, I want to get a head start, so I'm the first one to find something!"

While Daisy listened carefully to Dr. Theopolis's instructions, Donald dug faster and faster.

Suddenly Donald saw something shiny in the dirt. "Hey!" he called. "I've found a treasure!"

But when Dr. Theopolis brushed off Donald's discovery, it turned out to be a steel fork.

"The ancient Greeks usually ate with their fingers," said Dr. Theopolis. "This is probably from a tourist's picnic. But don't be discouraged," he added, seeing the disappointment on Donald's face. "Sometimes archaeologists dig for years before they turn up anything."

"Years!" Donald thought. He began digging even faster.

"Moderation, Donald," Daisy reminded him. "Take your time. Otherwise you'll wear yourself out or miss something important."

"Finding a buried treasure is what's important," Donald said. He tossed a piece of broken pottery out of his way.

After a while Donald decided to give up. "I don't think there really is anything buried here," he muttered to Daisy. "All I keep finding are pieces of old pottery," he complained, tossing another chunk on the pile.

Daisy looked at the pile of pottery pieces and burst out laughing.

"What's so funny?" Donald asked.

"Donald, you have found something!" Daisy said. "I'll bet that those pieces of pottery are important."

Daisy called Zena and Dr. Theopolis over to look at Donald's find. "It looks like these pieces are part of an ancient vase," Dr. Theopolis said. "It was probably used thousands of years ago."

"It doesn't look like a vase," Donald said. "Are you sure?"

"See how these pieces fit together, like a puzzle?" Dr. Theopolis asked, holding two pieces together. "Pottery is too delicate to survive for thousands of years without breaking."

They watched as Dr. Theopolis carefully showed them how the pieces of the vase fit together.

"Thousands of years ago someone made this vase and painted figures on it. Finding vases like this gives us an idea of what life was like in ancient times," Dr. Theopolis explained.

"This is a good discovery," the scientist declared. "Maybe you should think about becoming an archaeologist," he told Donald.

Donald thought about all the hard work he had done. "A little archaeology is fun," he said with a smile, "but I wouldn't want to do too much of it. You know me, moderation in all things."

Daisy just rolled her eyes as Zena laughed and laughed.

Did You Know…?

There are many different customs and places that make each country special. Do you remember some of the things below from the story?

Greece has more than a thousand islands that lie off its mainland. Some of the islands are bare and rocky, while others are covered with plants and trees. People come from all over the world to take cruises around the Greek islands.

The island of Rhodes has many wonderful sights. One sight you won't see, however, is the famous Colossus of Rhodes. This giant statue of a man straddled the island's harbor and stood more than one hundred feet tall. It was one of the Seven Wonders of the Ancient World, but it was destroyed by an earthquake many years ago.

Archaeologists in Greece have dug up many important things from the past, including ancient pottery, stone writing tablets, sculptures, and even entire temples and palaces. These buried treasures date back thousands of years and tell us how the ancient Greeks lived.

Some special Greek foods include lemon soup, grape leaves stuffed with rice or meat, and feta cheese, which is made from goat's milk.

The Olympic Games began in Olympia and were held there for over a thousand years. The first competition consisted of only one event—a foot race. The winner was presented with a wreath of olive leaves. The first modern Olympic Games were held in Athens, the capital of Greece, in 1896.

Greeks have dances for many occasions. There are fast, happy dances and slow, sad ones. Some dances are for men, and others are for women. One special dance, the Sailor's Dance, is done in a circle to slow music that gradually grows faster and faster.

Fishing is an important industry in Greece. Greek fishing boats haul in many different kinds of fish, as well as sponges, plantlike sea animals.

Our alphabet is based on the Greek alphabet. Zena has written the first two letters of the Greek alphabet, *alpha* and *beta*.

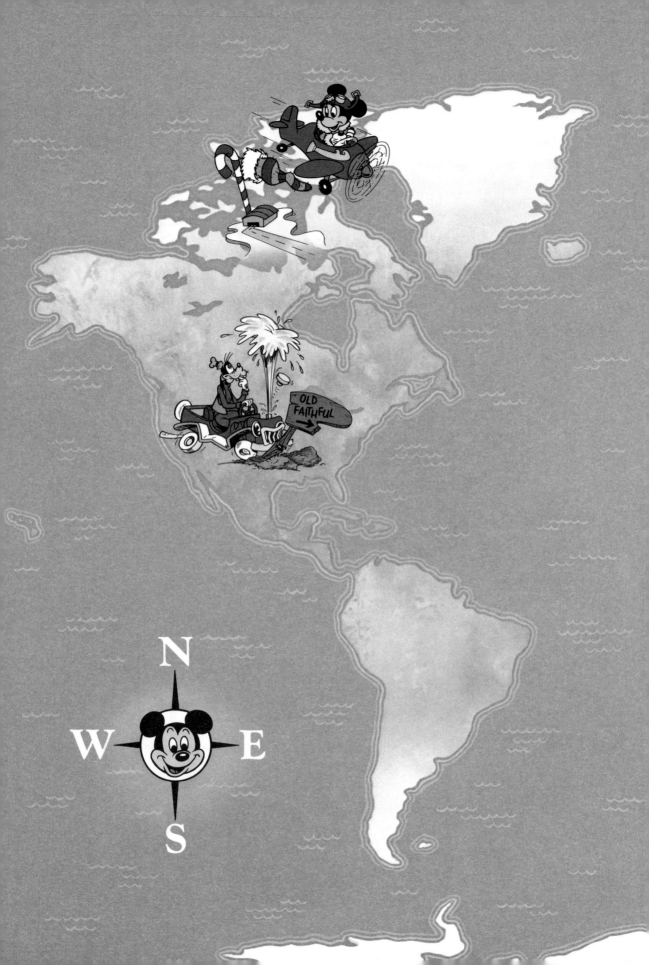